· MAY ·

· JUNE ·

· JULY ·

· NOVEMBER ·

· DECEMBER ·

· JANUARY ·

· AUGUST ·

· SEPTEMBER ·

· OCTOBER ·

· FEBRUARY ·

· MARCH ·

· APRIL ·

WILLIAM KITTEN

AND HIS

PICTURES AND STORY

by MARJORIE FLACK

HOUGHTON MIFFLIN COMPANY

The Riverside Press, Cambridge

ONCE there was a kitten, a little striped kitten, who was lost. It was lost on Pollywinkle Lane in the village of Pleasantville;

lost on a Monday morning
in May.

'Me-ew, me-ew, me-ew!' cried this little lost kitten, and it followed the people, coming and going, up and down Pollywinkle Lane.

It followed the Milkman.

It followed the Mailman.

It followed the Grocery boy.

But they paid no attention to the little lost kitten because they were all much too busy.

It followed the fathers
on their way to work.

It followed the children
on their way to school.

It followed the mothers
on their way to market.

But they paid no attention to the little
lost kitten because they were all much
too busy.

Then it followed a small boy named William. The kitten followed William up and down, and down and up the side walk on Pollywinkle Lane.

Now William was only four years old, so he was too young to be a Milkman.
He was too young to be a Postman.
He was too young to be a Grocery boy.
He was too young to be a father, and he was too young to go to the Pleasantville school.

So William was not so busy. He was not too busy to pay attention to this little lost kitten.

William stopped riding his scooter, and he patted the little kitten, and he said, 'Nice little kitty, where did you come from?'

But all the little kitten could say was 'Me-ew, me-ew!'

So William did not know that this kitten was lost.

" All morning long William
played with the kitten.

At noontime William's brother
Charles and his sister Nancy came home
from school.

'Hurry up, William!' they called,
'Hurry up, William, time for lunch!'

and they ran into their white house on Pollywinkle Lane.

'I'm coming, I'm coming!' called William,

and he ran into the house after them. And then what did that little kitten do, but run right into the house after William, before he had time to shut the door!

'My goodness me,' said their mother, 'William, wherever did you find that kitten?'

'But I didn't find him,' said William, 'he found me!'

'Me-ew, me-ew, me-ew!' cried the little kitten, and it sniffed the pleasant smell of food, 'Me-ew, me-ew!'

Then William knew,
      and his mother knew,
      and Nancy knew,
      and Charles knew,
         they all knew that
            this little kitten was hungry,
               and it was hungry
                  because it was lost!

'Poor little kitten!' they all said together, and then they gave it some warm milk for lunch, and it lapped it all up

until its tummy was as round as could be, and it no longer cried 'Me-ew, me-ew!' but sang, 'Prrrrrrr-prrrrrrr!'

'Please may I keep him?' William asked his mother, 'I will call him Peter, and I will take good care of him because he will belong to me.'

'But it may have a name already,' said his mother, 'and it may belong to someone else.'

'Oh, dear!' said William.

'Oh, dear!' said Nancy.

But Charles said, 'What shall we do?'

'Now let me think,' said their mother. 'You might put a notice in the paper, or you might put a note in the Post Office, but the quickest way I know is to take it to the Chief of Police at the Police Station after school this afternoon. Tell him William found it, and if it has no home we will give it one.'

So after lunch William took good care of the little kitten and he called it 'Peter' all the time because he liked that name. When Nancy and Charles came back from school they helped William put the kitten in a market basket.

And down they all went, down Polly-winkle Lane, on their way to Main street.

Then they passed by the Drug store. They passed by the Grocery store. They passed by the church, and they passed by the Post Office, until at last they came to the Police Station.

There they met the Chief of Police, and he said, 'How do you do, and what can I do for you today?'

'William found a kitten, sir,' said Charles.

'And it is here, sir,' said Nancy.

And she held the basket and William lifted the kitten out and put it on the desk.

'Well, well,' said the Chief of Police. 'Well, well, I'll look in my book and see if anyone has lost a kitten.'

So he looked in his book and he read:

-214-

May 4. Lost:- A striped kitten named Minnie. Phone Mrs. Finney at the Post Office. Reward.

May 6. Lost:- A kitten with white paws named Mouser. Phone Mr. Smith at the Grocery Store. Reward

May 8 Lost:- A black and gray kitten named May. Call Mr. Poole at the Drug Store. Reward.

'Well, well, well,' said the Chief of Police. 'There seems to be a lot of kittens lost lately.'

Then he looked at the kitten, and he saw that it had stripes, and he looked again and saw that it had white paws, and he looked again and saw that its colors were black and gray.

The Chief of Police said, 'Well, well, well! I guess I had better telephone all these people. I can't tell if this kitten is one of the three lost kittens or not. If it is, William will get a reward.'

So the Chief of Police telephoned Mrs. Finney at the Post Office, and Mr. Smith at the Grocery store, and Mr. Poole at the Drug store, and they all said they would come right over.

First came Mrs. Finney, and she looked at the kitten and she said, 'Yes, there is my little Minnie! My sister gave her to me last Monday, and Minnie stayed with me all Tuesday, but she ran away on Wednesday!'

Then along came Mr. Poole, and he said, 'Yes, that kitten is May. She came to me on Saturday but she ran away on Sunday!'

Then in came Mr. Smith, and as
soon as he saw the kitten he said, 'Yes,
it is Mouser. I found her at the store
on Thursday
but
she ran away
on Friday!'

'Well, well,' said the Chief of Police. 'Mrs. Finney, you have found your kitten; Mr. Smith, you have found your kitten; and Mr. Poole, you have found your kitten, so that makes three rewards for William, and I can cross out all three notices in my book!'

'But they are all the same kitten!' said Mr. Smith.

'And it is only one kitten!' said Mrs. Finney.

'So whose kitten is it?' asked Mr. Poole.

And William said, 'My mother said if it had no home we would give it a home, sir.'

'But this kitten has three homes!' said the Chief of Police.

Then Mrs. Finney said, 'I wanted a

cat to keep me company, but I will give Minnie to William for my reward.'

And Mr. Smith said, 'I wanted a cat to keep the mice away, but I will give Mouser to William for my reward.'

And Mr. Poole said, 'I wanted a cat to help tend the Drug store, but I will give May to William for my reward.'

'Well, well,' said the Chief of Police. 'Now William has three rewards, and I can cross out the notices in my book,' and so he did, and he wrote 'Found' after each one of them, and then he said to William, 'Now you can take your kitten home with you, and watch out that it stays at home.'

William said 'Thank you,' to Mrs. Finney and to Mr. Smith and to Mr. Poole and to the kind Chief of Police.

Then Nancy and Charles and William took the little kitten home to live with them in their white house on Pollywinkle Lane.

William always took very good care of his kitten, and it never ran away. He always called it Peter, although he knew its real name was Peter Minnie Mouser May.

Peter stayed at home with William a whole year.

Peter stayed with William all through the months of —

MAY

JUNE

JULY

· AUGUST ·

SEPTEMBER

· OCTOBER ·

NOVEMBER

· DECEMBER ·

JANUARY

· FEBRUARY ·

MARCH

· APRIL ·

until another May came.   And William was no longer four years old because he was five years old and going to school. And Peter was no longer a little kitten but a large, handsome cat.

Then early one morning in the month of May, when William called, 'Here, Peter, here, Peter, come get your breakfast!' no Peter came.

William called again, 'Here, Peter, Peter, Peter, Peter, here, Peter, Peter!' and still no Peter came. Then William said, 'Oh, dear, oh, dear, Peter has run away!'

But just then William heard a strange little squeaking noise coming from Peter's basket near the stove in the kitchen.

He looked in the basket,
   and there William saw

three tiny little kittens,
    three new little kittens,
        all cuddled up with their mother,
            and their mother was Peter!

One of these kittens was striped, and so William named it Minnie, and one had white paws, and so William named it Mouser, and the other one was black and gray, and so William named it May.

Peter took good care of her three little kittens, and they grew larger and stronger every day, and then one day when they were old enough to leave their mother, William put —

Minnie

and Mouser

and May

in the market basket.
Then William and Charles and Nancy took the basket full of kittens down Pollywinkle Lane and down to Main street.

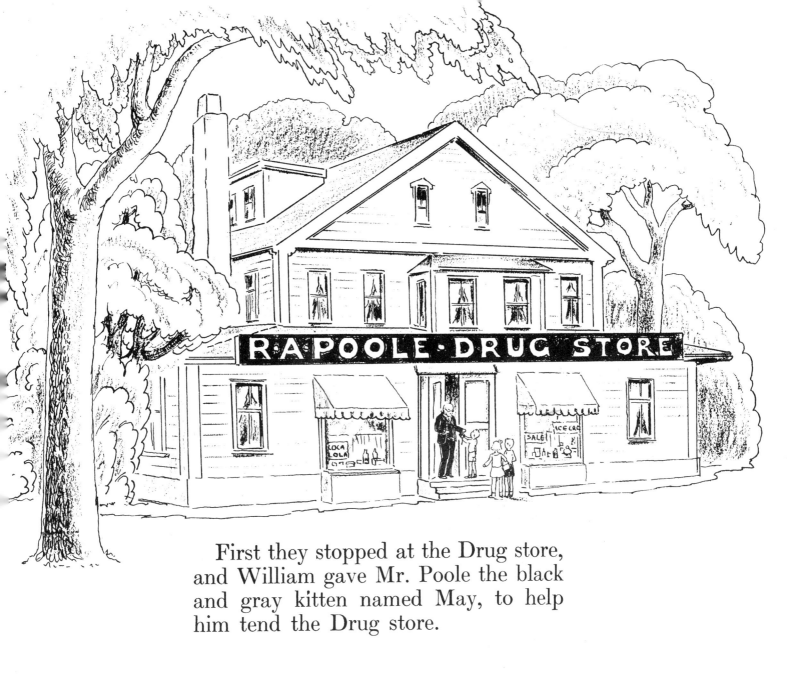

First they stopped at the Drug store,
and William gave Mr. Poole the black
and gray kitten named May, to help
him tend the Drug store.

Then they stopped at the Grocery store, and William gave Mr. Smith the kitten with white paws named Mouser, to help keep the mice away.

Then they stopped at the Post Office, and William gave Mrs. Finney the striped kitten named Minnie, to keep her company. And —

Mr. Poole
and Mr. Smith
and Mrs. Finney
were very pleased.

And so was William.

·MAY·

·JUNE·

·JULY·

·NOVEMBER·

·DECEMBER·

·JANUARY·